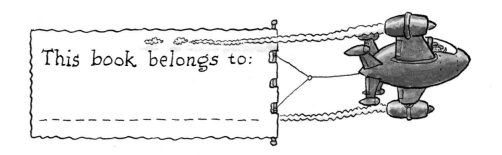

This book belongs to:

_____

To Jenny,
Josh and Connor,
with love.

First published in Great Britain in 2010 by Andersen Press Ltd.,

20 Vauxhall Bridge Road, London SW1V 2SA.

Published in Australia by Random House Australia Pty.,

Level 3, 100 Pacific Highway, North Sydney, NSW 2060.

Copyright © John Fardell, 2010.

The rights of John Fardell to be identified as the author and illustrator

of this work have been asserted by him in accordance with

the Copyright, Designs and Patents Act, 1988.

All rights reserved.

Colour separated in Switzerland by Photolitho AG, Zürich.

Printed and bound in Singapore by Tien Wah Press.

John Fardell has used pen-and-ink and watercolour in this book.

10   9   8   7   6   5   4   3   2

British Library Cataloguing in Publication Data available.

ISBN 978 1 84939 014 9 (hardback)

ISBN 978 1 84939 147 4 (paperback)

This book has been printed on acid-free paper

JEREMIAH JELLYFISH

FLIES HIGH!

John Fardell

ANDERSEN PRESS

Jeremiah Jellyfish . . .

lived with
his mother
and father
and brothers
and sisters . . .

and with
his aunts
and uncles
and
grandmother
and
grandfather . . .

and with hundreds and hundreds of other jellyfish
in a huge shoal.

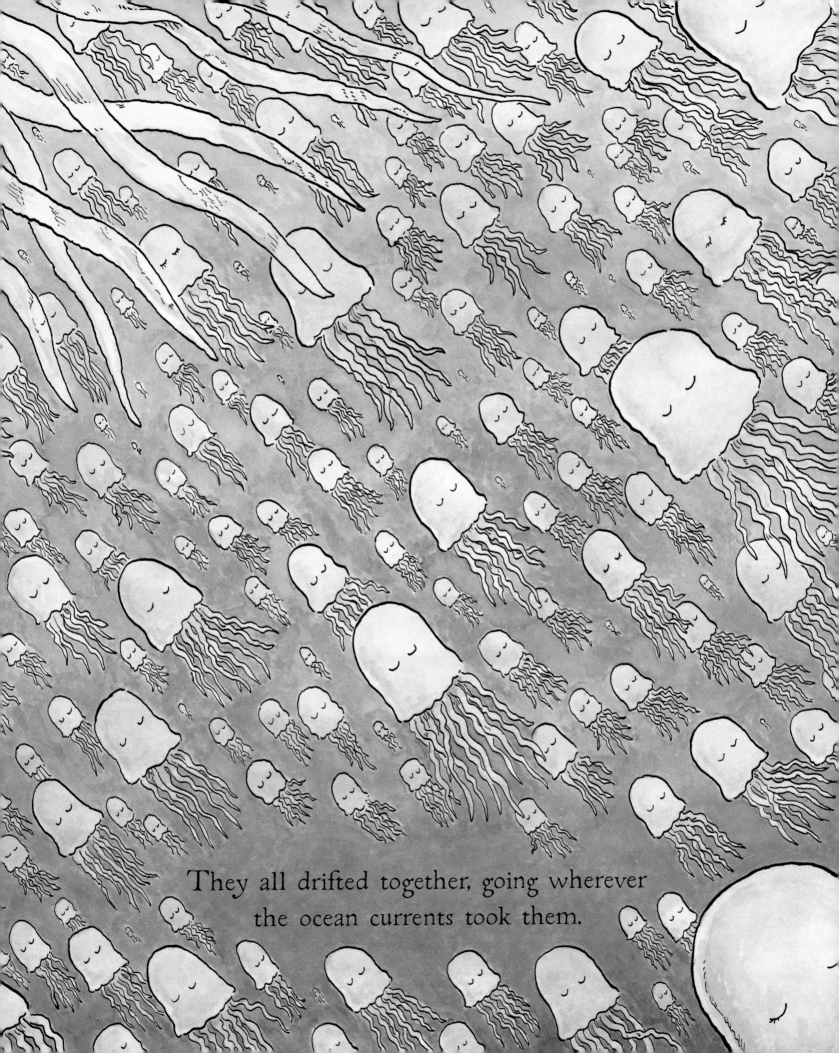

They all drifted together, going wherever
the ocean currents took them.

"Why do I have to drift?" asked Jeremiah one day. "Why can't I swim away to see the world?"

"Because you're a jellyfish," said his mother and father. "Drifting is what we do."

"If you swim away to see the world," said his brothers and sisters, "the porpoises will eat you."

"If you swim away to see the world," said his aunts and uncles, "the jellyfishermen will catch you."

But his grandfather said, "Don't listen to them, Jeremiah! When I was your age, *I* dreamed of swimming away to see the world. But I never had the courage. You go for it!"

So Jeremiah turned and swam against the ocean current. He swam out past the edges of the jellyfish shoal and, for the first time in his life, he found himself . . .

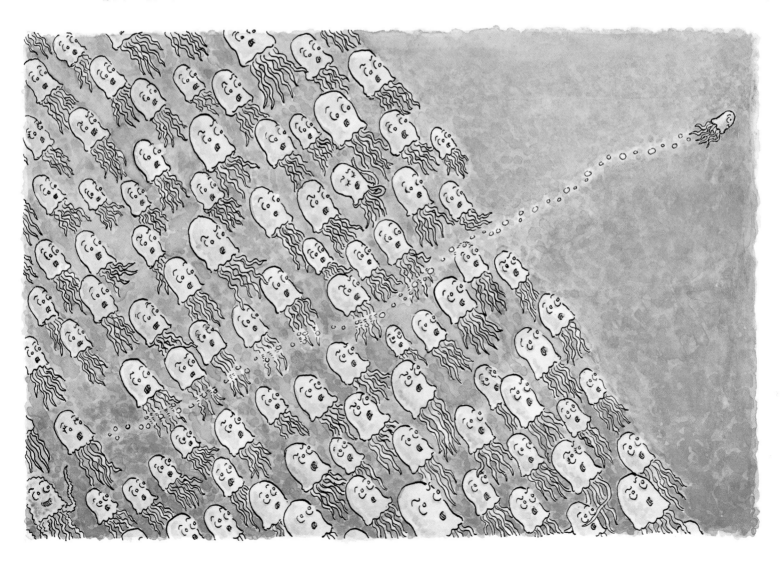

alone.

Jeremiah swam and swam.

He didn't get eaten by porpoises . . .

and he didn't get caught by the jellyfishermen.

Eventually, Jeremiah reached the shore.

Near the shore was a beach hut. Jeremiah decided to look inside.

He found a man,
sleeping.

"Uh! Who's there?"
cried the man,
waking suddenly.

"I'm Jeremiah Jellyfish," said Jeremiah. "Good morning."

"Is it morning already?" said the man. "I only came down here
to watch the sunset. I must get back to the city and go to work."

"What do you do?" asked Jeremiah.

"I'm a high-flyer," said the man. "I'm the Director-in-Chief
of the biggest rocket plane company in the world."

"Wow! That sounds exciting!" said Jeremiah.

"I suppose it is," said the man,
"but it's worn me out. What do you do?"

"Oh, we jellyfish just drift around in the
sea, mostly," said Jeremiah.

"Wow! That sounds relaxing!"
said the man. "Let's swap!"

So the man arranged everything. Very soon, a company rocket plane arrived, bringing a diving-suit for the man.

"Good luck! Have fun!" he called, as he drifted off beneath the waves.

The rocket plane took off, and in no time at all . . .

Jeremiah Jellyfish was flying high.

Soon he arrived at his office.

Over the next few weeks, Jeremiah Jellyfish dictated e-mails . . .

dealt with phone calls . . .

flew to international conferences . . .

and took important business decisions.

He was very good at being a high-flyer.

Meanwhile, the man drifted happily with the jellyfish shoal.

He was very good at drifting.

One afternoon, Jeremiah got a phone call from the man.

"Hi! How are things going?" the man asked.

"Fine!" said Jeremiah. "But I could do with a bit of a rest now. How's life in the sea?"

"Fine!" said the man. "I'm more relaxed than I've ever been. But I'm getting a bit bored now. How about swapping back for a bit?"

That evening, Jeremiah arrived back at the seashore.

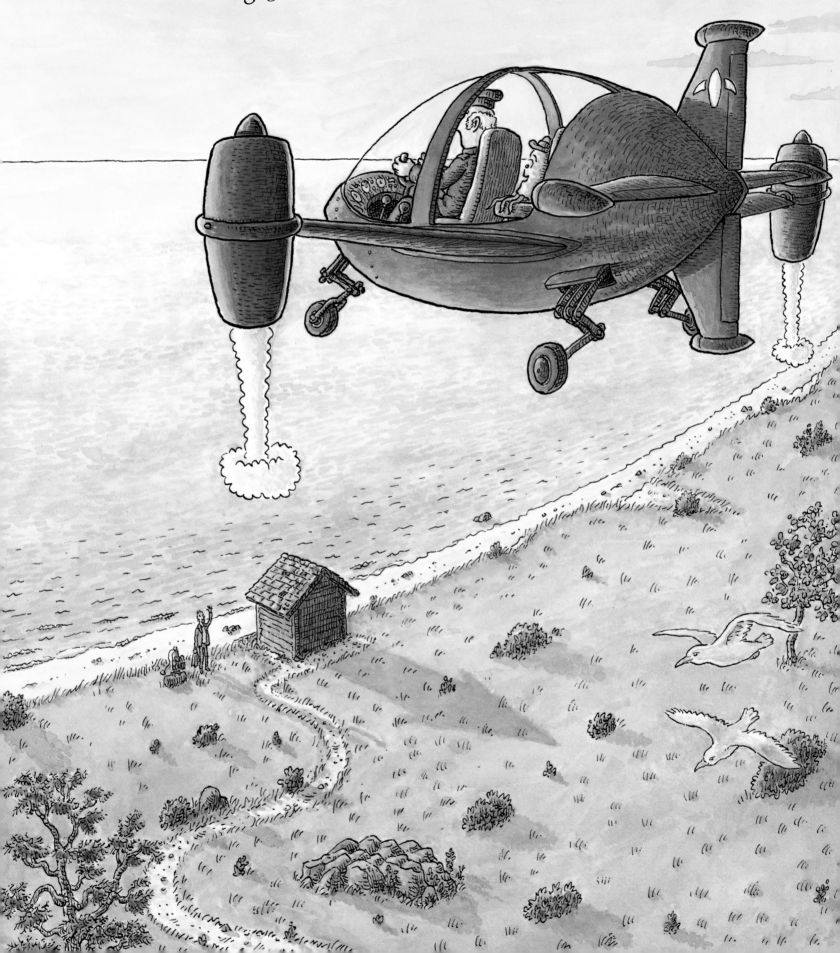

"Let me know when you want another change," said the man. "It's fun being a high-flyer sometimes, isn't it?"

"It is," said Jeremiah.

"But

sometimes,

it's

good

to

just

d r i f t . . ."

Other books you might enjoy:

9781849390477

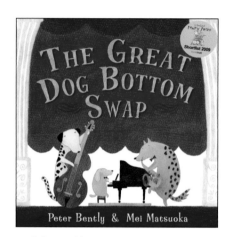

9781842709887

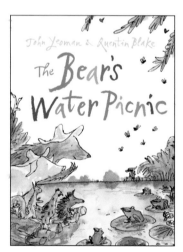

9781849390040

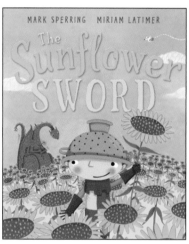

9781849390774

9781842709481